D0405986

Other chapter books you might enjoy:

The **Veterans Day Visitor**

2nd-Grade Friends

The Veterans Day Visitor

Peter Catalanotto
and Pamela Schembri

Henry Holt and Company ★ New York

Henry Holt and Company, LLC

Publishers since 1866

175 Fifth Avenue, New York, New York 10010

www.HenryHoltKids.com

Henry Holt® is a registered trademark of Henry Holt and Company, LLC.

Library of Congress Cataloging-in-Publication Data
Catalanotto, Peter.
The Veterans Day visitor / Peter Catalanotto and Pamela Schembri.—1st ed.
p.   cm. — (Second-grade friends; bk. 3)
Summary: Second-grader Emily worries that her grandfather,
who has narcolepsy, will fall asleep when he visits her class to talk
about Veterans Day.
ISBN-13: 978-0-8050-7840-4 / ISBN-10: 0-8050-7840-1
[1. Veterans Day—Fiction. 2. Grandfathers—Fiction.
3. Schools—Fiction.]
I. Schembri, Pamela. II. Title.
PZ7.C26878Ve 2008   [Fic]—dc22   2007040938

First Edition—2008
Printed in the United States of America on acid-free paper. ∞

1 3 5 7 9 10 8 6 4 2

To Rolling Thunder, New York Chapter 3—
Thank you for keeping my father's dream alive.

Special thanks to the students at Temple Hill Academy
—P. S.

For Noreen and Alan
—P. C.

The Veterans Day Visitor

Contents

Chapter 1

Pop-Pop's House

Emily never jumped in leaves.

They were dirty.

They might be wet.

Bugs crawled in them.

At Emily's grandparents' house, there were piles and piles of leaves. Emily and her best friend, Vinni, were visiting after school on a sunny November day.

"Watch me!" Vinni shouted. She ran and jumped into a mountain of leaves.

Emily wrinkled her nose. "Aren't they itchy?"

"No!" said Vinni. "It's fun!"

"Ick," said Emily.

Vinni shook her head. "You are so weird." She threw a bunch of leaves at Emily.

Emily laughed.

"You know, girls, different people like different things." Emily and Vinni stopped. Emily's Pop-Pop was standing behind them. He leaned against his rake.

"For example, *you*, Vincetta—"

"Vinni," interrupted Vinni.

Pop-Pop started again. "For example, *you*, Vinni"—he pointed right at her— "you like wearing fancy hair clips, fancy shoes, and fancy pants."

"So does Emily," Vinni said.

"Exactly," said Pop-Pop. "Without the hair clips."

"So how is that different?" Emily asked.

Pop-Pop stroked his chin. "No hair clips."

Vinni's mouth was open. She raised one eyebrow and looked at Emily. Emily shrugged. The girls waited.

"You know," said Pop-Pop, "it's good that people are different. For example, next Monday is Veterans Day." Pop-Pop loved to talk. "Different people will

18

celebrate in different ways. Some people will hang a flag. Some will go to a parade. Others will remember loved ones quietly at home."

"What's a veteran?" asked Emily.

"It's a doctor for dogs," said Vinni.

"That's a veterinarian," said Emily.

Pop-Pop was shocked. He put down his rake. "You don't *know*?" He pointed at both of them. "You don't know about the people who helped keep our country free? Don't you . . . I can't believe . . . second grade?"

Suddenly Pop-Pop stopped talking.
His knees buckled.

The girls couldn't move.

He bit his lip. He steadied himself.

"I need to lie down." Pop-Pop went
to the hammock and fell fast asleep.

Chapter 2

🇺🇸

Sleepy Stories

"What happened to him?" asked Vinni.

"Ummm . . . well . . . nothing," said Emily. "Let's jump in the leaves!"

"WAIT!" cried Vinni. "Is he dead?"

Emily blushed. "No. He's asleep."

"WHY?"

"He has narcolepsy," Emily explained. "It makes him fall asleep."

"Really? Anytime? Anywhere?"

"Yep."

"Weird! He was just talking to us and then . . ." Vinni closed her eyes and snored.

"Yep," said Emily. "Asleep."

"How did he get narc-o-sleepy?"

"Narcolepsy," said Emily. "He was born with it."

"Can I catch it?"

"No. You have it or you don't." Emily sat down in the grass.

"Does it ever happen when he's eating?" Vinni asked.

"Sometimes. Once we had to slide his plate of spaghetti away from him."

"Gross!" said Vinni.

"It's not so bad. In fact, sometimes—" Emily stopped.

"WHAT?"

"Nothing."

"Come on! Tell me! I won't tell anyone! I promise!" Vinni crossed her heart with her finger. Then she spit in her hand and held it out for Emily to shake.

"Ewww!" squealed Emily. She pushed Vinni's hand back. "All right!

I'll tell you. Just don't ever do THAT
again!"

Vinni wiped her hand on her pants.

Emily took a deep breath. "Sometimes he tells stories when he's asleep."

"Wow!" said Vinni. "Would he do
it now?"

"Let's go see," said Emily.

The girls ran to the hammock.

"Pop-Pop," Emily whispered.

"Huh?" Pop-Pop said. He was still asleep.

"Pop-Pop, what about your dog, King?" asked Emily.

"Oh, the dog," Pop-Pop said, "on the magazine."

The girls' eyes were wide. Emily nodded.

"That was the day he swam to Ice Cream Island, for the bee's nest . . . because he was known for honey."

Emily smiled and poked Vinni.

"You know," Pop-Pop said, "ice cream made with honey is better than ice cream in a cone."

Vinni laughed.

Pop-Pop woke up. "What? Emily? Oh." He sat up.

"As I was saying, I'm coming to your school to tell your whole class about Veterans Day."

"Really, Pop-Pop? That would be great! I think my teacher, Mr. Marvin, would like that."

"Maybe you'll tell another sleepy story!" said Vinni.

Emily looked at Vinni. Then she looked at Pop-Pop. Maybe it wasn't such a great idea, she thought.

Chapter 3

🇺🇸

What If?

Mr. Marvin was excited. "Our guest speaker, Mr. Moore, will be here in thirty minutes. I want the room to look nice." He clapped his hands. "Melissa, set up the chairs. The rest of you, finish your snack and clean up."

Vinni drank her chocolate milk and opened her journal. "Hey, Emily. Can I borrow a marker?"

Emily handed her a pretzel stick.

"Ah, pretzel! My favorite color!"

"Huh?" asked Emily. "Oh. Sorry."

Vinni reached over and took a green marker. "What's wrong with you today?" she asked. "You're weirder than ever!"

Emily put her head on her desk. "What if . . . when Pop-Pop starts talking . . . he gets . . ."

"Boring?" asked Vinni.

"No, not boring," said Emily. "What if he gets . . . sleepy?"

"That would be cool!" said Vinni. "We'd hear another kooky story."

"That would NOT be cool," said Emily. "Everyone will laugh."

"Oh, yeah," said Vinni. She pushed her journal aside and laid her head on her arms.

The girls looked at each other.

Maria sharpened her pencil.

Robert blew his nose.

"Don't worry," said Vinni. "I won't *let* him fall asleep. I'll ask him lots of questions."

Emily raised an eyebrow.

"It's going to be okay, you'll see." Vinni patted Emily on the back. "Now finish eating your markers."

Chapter 4

The Visit

"Emily," said Mr. Marvin, "would you please introduce our guest?"

Pop-Pop sat in the big rocking chair. His whole face was smiling.

Emily tried to smile back. She went to the front of the room and said quickly, "This is my Pop-Pop. He was a veteran." She went back to her chair.

Pop-Pop looked at Emily. He was a little surprised. "Okay," he rubbed his hands together. "Today I'm here to tell you about veterans and Veterans Day. Emily told you I was a veteran. Actually, I *am* a veteran. I *was* a soldier. Soldiers become veterans." He nodded at the class.

"Are those medals for shooting people?" Joey asked.

Vinni said, "Let him talk, Joey! And next time raise your hand!"

Now Mr. Marvin looked surprised.

Pop-Pop continued. "Well, Joey, I'm glad you asked. Not all veterans fought in wars. These medals are for tasks I've completed."

"Like a cub scout!" yelled Sam.

Pop-Pop pointed right at him. "Exactly."

Pop-Pop stood up. "Some soldiers *do* fight in battles. When I was in the army, our country was not at war. But I'm *still* a veteran. Veterans are people who served in the armed forces—even if they didn't fight in battle."

"My aunt Josie used to fly helicopters in the navy," said Emmanuel.

"*She's* a veteran." Pop-Pop nodded.

Anell said, "My father's friend died in a war."

Pop-Pop took off his hat and placed it over his heart. He spoke quietly. "He's a veteran. A fallen veteran. Veterans who have died have another special day—Memorial Day."

Pop-Pop's knees buckled. He steadied himself.

Emily looked around the room.
Everyone was staring at Pop-Pop. She
saw Pop-Pop's eyes blink hard. Emily
elbowed Vinni.

Vinni waved her hand wildly and asked, "How did you get your buttons so shiny?"

Pop-Pop sat down in the big rocking chair, but didn't answer.

Emily jumped up. She quickly moved to the front of the room.

"My Pop-Pop taught me to respect
fallen veterans with a moment of
silence." She lowered her head like
Pop-Pop's.

Mr. Marvin motioned for the class
to do the same.

Emily squeezed her Pop-Pop's
shoulder. "Was that long enough,
Pop-Pop?"

"Huh?" he asked. "Emily?" He looked
around the room. He looked at Emily.
She was grinning.
"Yes," he said, "that's long enough."

Chapter 5

🇺🇸

Thank You, Pop-Pop

The following week Emily visited Pop-Pop at his house.

"Did Mr. Marvin give my special flag to your principal?" Pop-Pop asked Emily.

"Oh, boy!" Emily exclaimed. "Did he ever!"

Emily sat next to Pop-Pop. She showed him her school's newsletter. "Look, here's your name! Here's a picture of your special flag. Pop-Pop, you're famous!"

Pop-Pop smiled. He was pleased. "Well, I did feel like a movie star when I got so many letters from your class this week." He chuckled warmly.

"Did you have a favorite letter?"
Emily teased.

Pop-Pop smiled and ruffled his
granddaughter's hair. "What do you
think?"

Dear Mr. Moore,

Thank you for visiting our class.
I liked when you told us about
veterans.
I learned that all veterans don't
always fight in wars.
I'm glad you didn't fight in a war,
so you could come to our class.
I liked at the end when you said if you
love your freedom, thank a veteran.
Next Veterans Day, I will. Even if
I have to wake him up first.

I love you, Pop-Pop,
Emily

Author's Note

The character Pop-Pop is based on my father, Tony Schembri. As a child, I was often asked when friends came to visit, "What's narc-o-sleepy?" My father had narcolepsy, and like Pop-Pop, he would fall asleep at the strangest times. My favorite stories were those he told somewhere between sleepiness and dreamtime.

As a narcoleptic, my father was lucky. He was always able to work, he was able to drive safely, and he served in the military.

His symptoms didn't appear until later in his life. It was a little confusing at first, but we learned to understand his condition. He never let narcolepsy stop him from accomplishing his goals, especially in his work with the veterans.

My father was an educator, a leader, and a political activist. He was a major force behind the creation of the U.S. Postal Service's Purple Heart Stamp, and he worked with local senators to create the Purple Heart Hall of Honor. During the last twelve years of his life, my father shared the stories of veterans with anyone who would listen: students, teachers, even congressional leaders. His stories helped change lives, and his own life serves as an example of how people with disabilities can still accomplish great success. It is an honor to bring his message to a much wider audience.

For more information about veterans, you can visit the home page of Rolling Thunder at www.rollingthunder1.com. The local chapter may be able to provide a speaker like Pop-Pop. For classroom activities and speakers, AMVETS offers an educational program at its Web site: www.amvets.org.

—Pamela Schembri